E-MERGENCY!

THE CAST

A B C D
E F G H I
J K L M
N O P Q
R S T U
V W X Y Z
? !

THE OTHER CAST

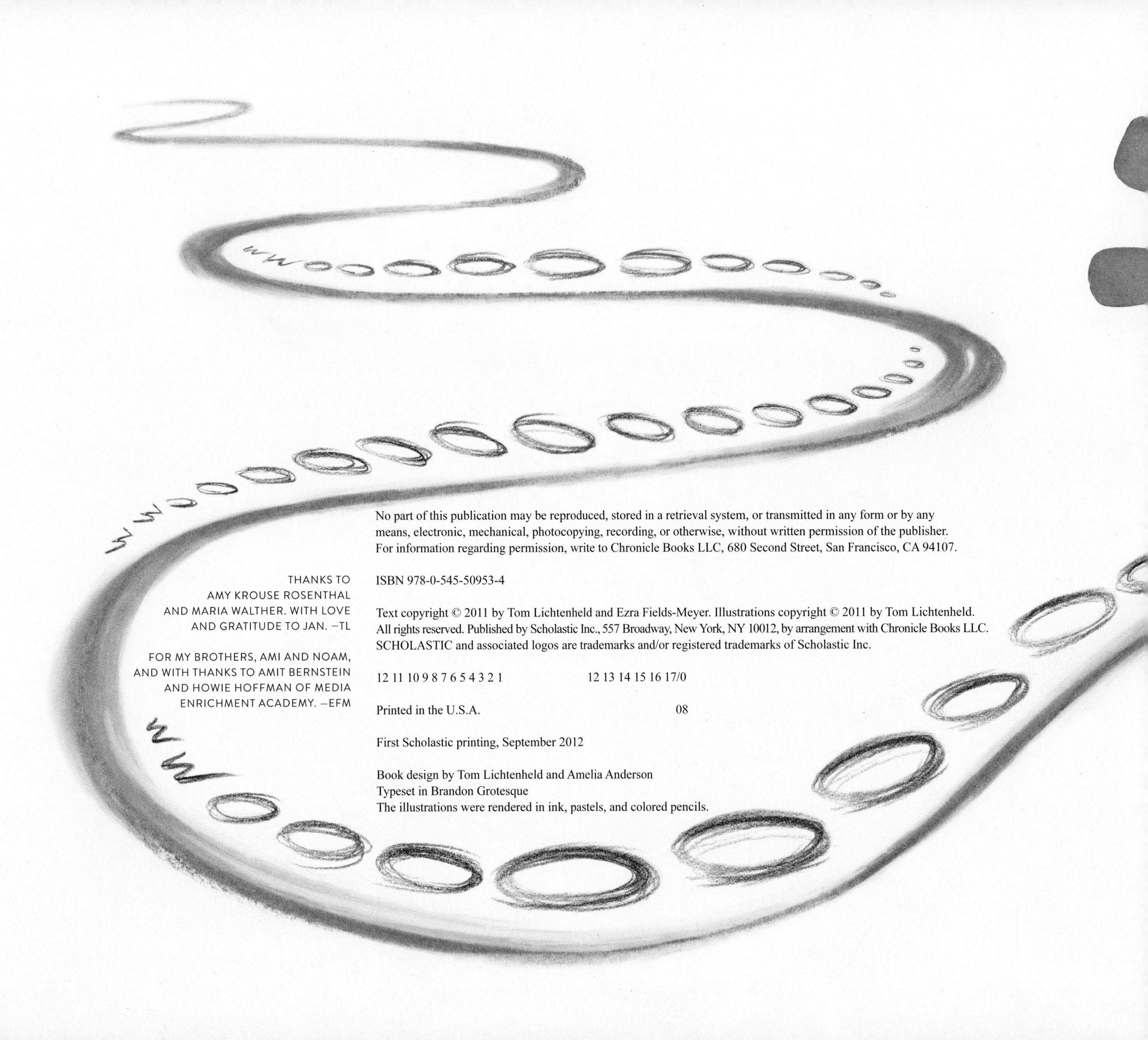

THANKS TO
AMY KROUSE ROSENTHAL
AND MARIA WALTHER. WITH LOVE
AND GRATITUDE TO JAN. –TL

FOR MY BROTHERS, AMI AND NOAM,
AND WITH THANKS TO AMIT BERNSTEIN
AND HOWIE HOFFMAN OF MEDIA
ENRICHMENT ACADEMY. –EFM

ISBN 978-0-545-50953-4

12 11 10 9 8 7 6 5 4 3 2 1 12 13 14 15 16 17/0

Printed in the U.S.A. 08

First Scholastic printing, September 2012

Book design by Tom Lichtenheld and Amelia Anderson
Typeset in Brandon Grotesque
The illustrations were rendered in ink, pastels, and colored pencils.

E-MERGENCY!

SCHOLASTIC INC.

TOM LICHTENHELD
EZRA FIELDS-MEYER

ALL THE LETTERS LIVED
TOGETHER IN A BIG HOUSE.

I LOVE THESE OLD COMIC BOOKS!
ME, TOO!
SO, SOMETIMES YOU'RE A CONSONANT?
AND SOMETIMES YOU'RE A VOWEL?
YEP! I BOUNCE BACK AND FORTH!
HEY! WE WANT A KITE, TOO!
PIPE DOWN! I'M TRYING TO SLEEP!
DOES THIS SERIF MAKE MY BUTT LOOK BIG?
GEE, I'M SO GLAD YOU LIKE MY PARTY!
IT'S T-RIFFIC!
I'M QUITE USELESS WITHOUT YOU, U!
WE'LL ALWAYS BE TOGETHER!
THIS ISN'T A VERY GOOD REPORT CARD.
MMM... OUR FAVORITE!
SPAGHETTIOs!
JUST BE.

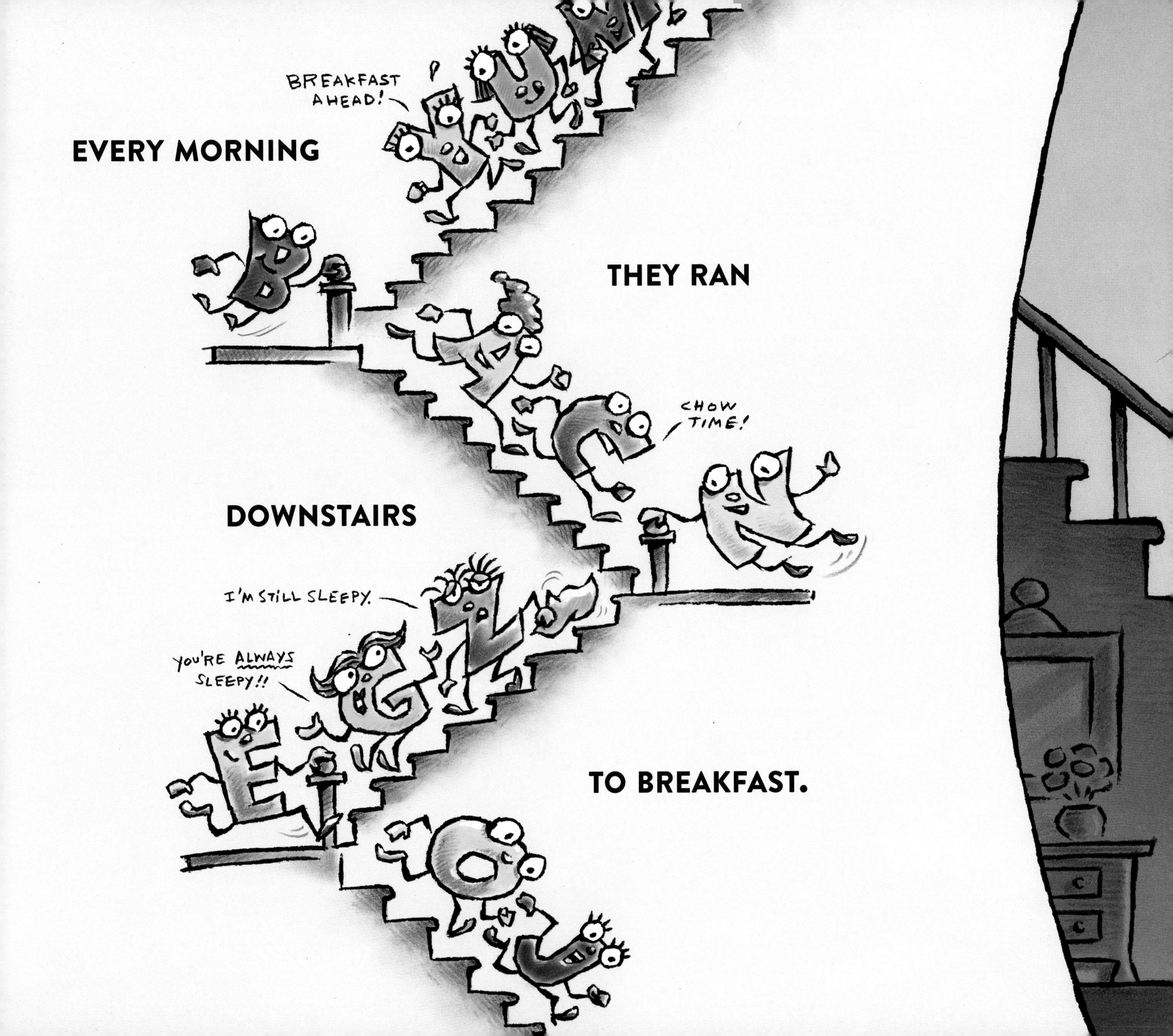
EVERY MORNING
BREAKFAST AHEAD!
THEY RAN
CHOW TIME!
DOWNSTAIRS
I'M STILL SLEEPY.
YOU'RE ALWAYS SLEEPY!!
TO BREAKFAST.

EEEEEE!
ONE MORNING, E CAME DOWN THE STAIRS A LITTLE TOO FAST.
oOO!

EVERYONE CAME RUNNING TO SEE WHAT HAPPENED.

AS ALWAYS, A TOOK ACTION.

THE **EMTs** RUSHED IN WITH AN **IV**,
READY TO PERFORM **CPR**.

THEN THEY GOT HER READY TO GO TO THE **ER.**

MD
TAKE TWO ASPIRIN AND CALL US IN THE A.M.!
wwWoOOOOOO....
AFTER THE AMBULANCE EXITED,
A ASSEMBLED THE ALPHABET.
SOMEONE IS GOING TO HAVE TO TAKE THE PLACE OF E WHILE SHE GETS BETTER.
O, YOU'RE THE OBVIOUS OPTION, BECAUSE YOU'RE SO WELL-ROUNDED.

But I'm SOoOo Busy! Why can't one of the consonants help out?

Don't be obnoxious, O. You know the consonants just speak gibberish without us vowels!
AEIOU
Y
BFF JK
NP BTW
BCNU
FWIW
RBTL TLC
THX
GE

So, NO ONE can use E, including US?

EGADS!

That's right. Starting right NOW, it's O instead of E.

That's it, poriod.

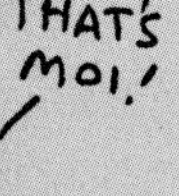
That's moi!

A AND EXCLAMATION MARK MADE THE BIG ANNOUNCEMENT.

D AND C WENT TO WASHINGTON TO ALERT THE U.S. GOVERNMENT.
WO NOOD FULL GOVORNMONT COOPORATION, INCLUDING THO OPA, THO FCC, THO FDIC, NASA, FOMA, AND OSHA!
OVORYBODY MUST FOLLOW OUR INSTRUCTIONS ABOUT THO LOTTOR TO THO LOTTOR!
THIS WON'T BO OASY!

AND THE REST OF THE LETTERS TALKED IT UP ON THE TALK SHOWS.

THO
O
SHOW
LOOK AT MO!
I'M ON TV!
Hi, mom!
I HAVO TO GO TO
THO BATHROOM.
AGAIN?!
YOU TWO
SHOULDN'T SIT
TOGOTHOR!

O DID HIS BEST FILLING IN FOR E,

BUT THE RESULTS WERE QUITE CONFUSING.

ROOSOVOLT OLOMONTARY SCHOOL
WOLCOMO STUDONTS!
SPOLLING TOST TODAY!
PTO MOOTING - WOD.

TODAY'S DOLICIOUS LUNCH
MOATLOAF
GROON SALAD
POAS
DOSSORT-
JOLLO AND
POACHOS
CAFOTORIA
BLOCH!

SPOOD
LIMIT
30
GOODYOAR
OAT AT MOL'S
DRINK
COLA
JAN'S
SHO
SHOP
ICO CROAM
ACMO
SIGN
CO.
TARGOT

FOR RONT
DANCO LOSSONS
OLM ST.
TANT LOTTOR HURT!!
"O" DOOS DOUBLO DUTY!
OL'S DINOR
HAM URGORS • FRIOS •
ONO WAY
MOL'S
BOOP BOOP!

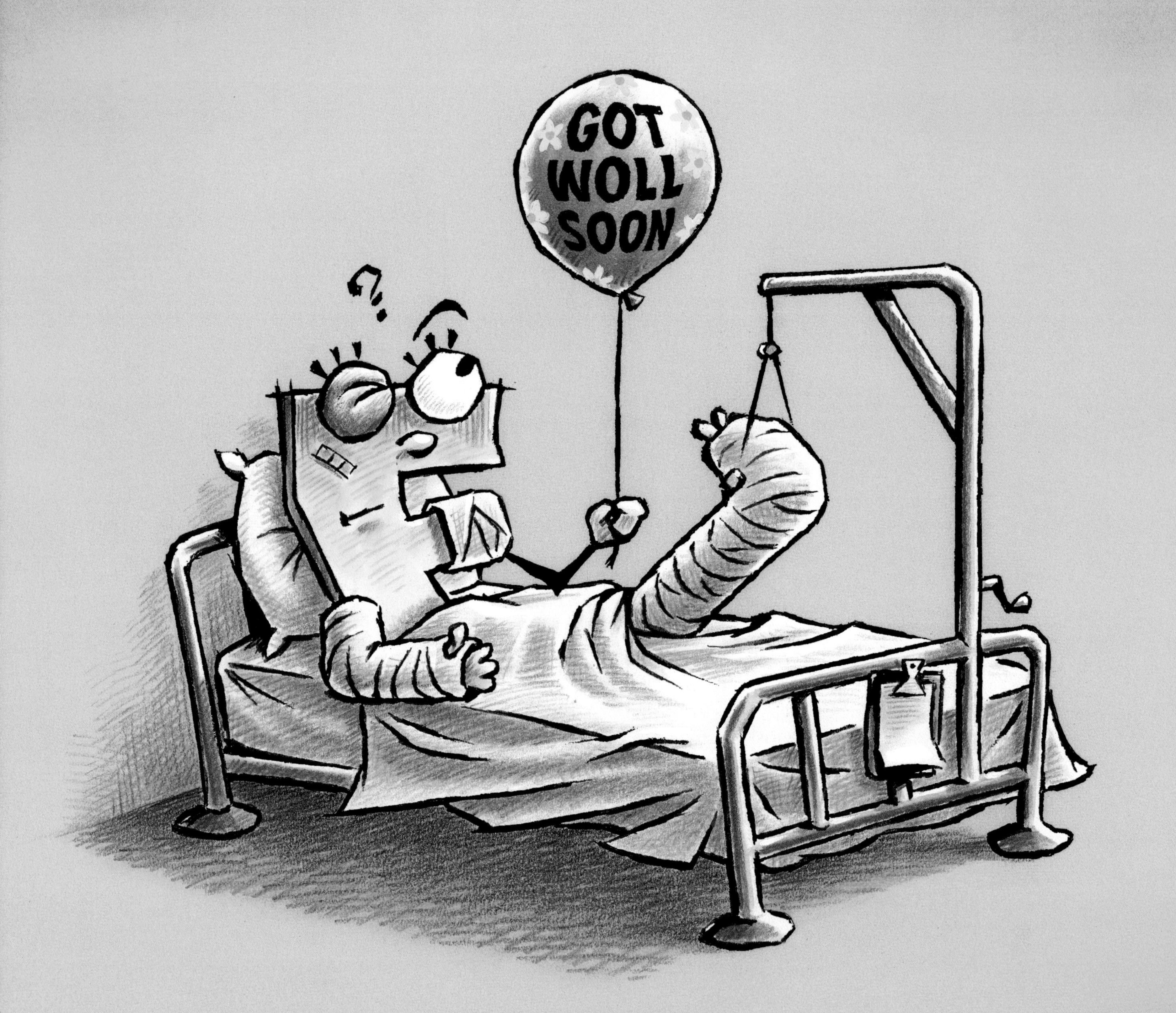
GOT
WOLL
SOON

TO MAKE MATTERS WORSE, E WASN'T GETTING BETTER. THE MDs COULDN'T FIGURE OUT WHY.

A DECIDED THEY NEEDED TO TAKE A TRIP TO SPREAD THE WORD ABOUT THE LETTER.

I'M TAKING IT ALL!
I'M WORKING OUT A PLAN!
I'M IN!
I'M PACKOD!
I'M OXCITOD!!

THEY TRAVELED NEAR . . .

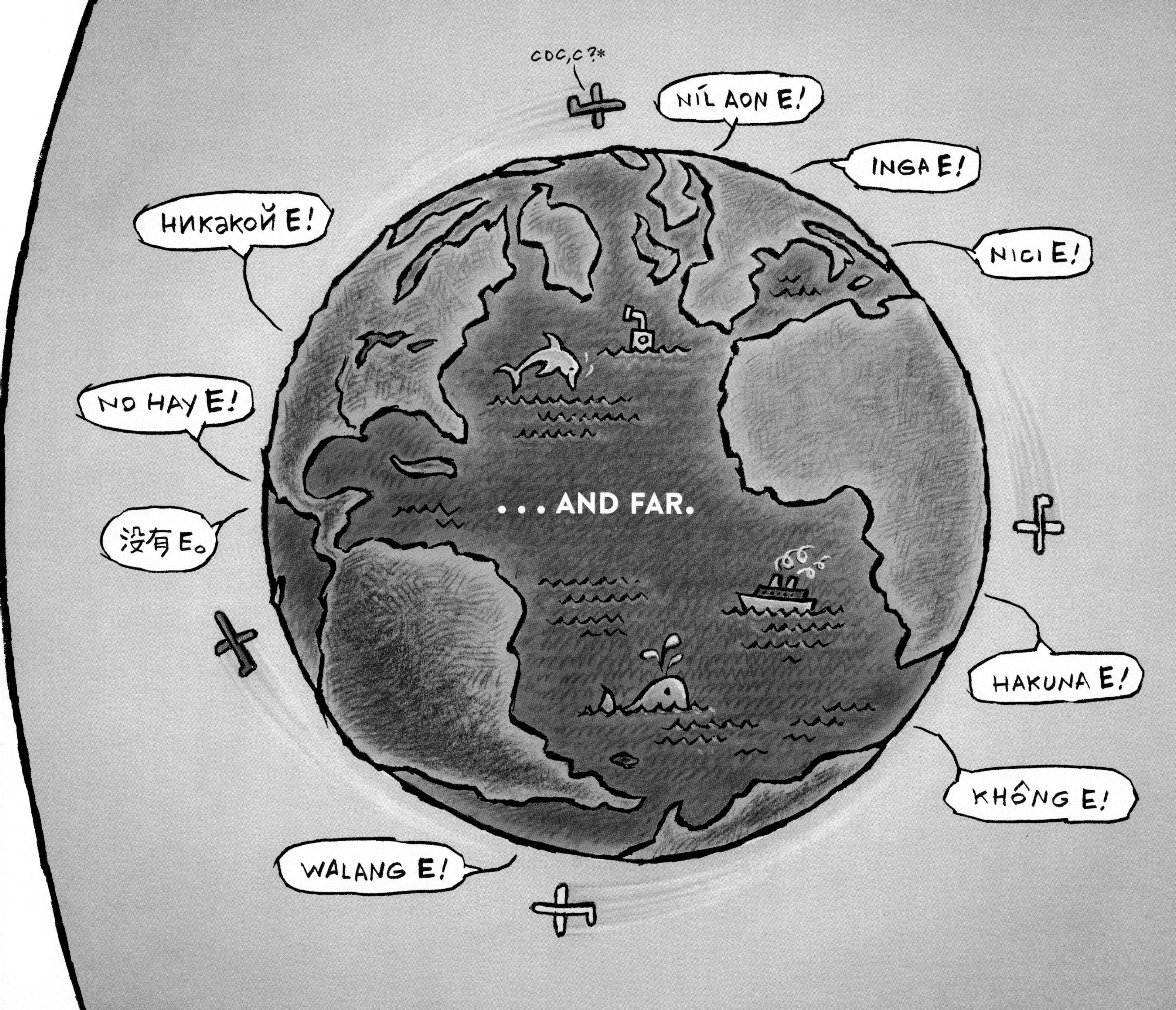

. . . AND FAR.

*THANKS TO WILLIAM STEIG

WHEN THEY GOT HOME, E STILL WASN'T RECOVERED.

THE LETTERS HAD A PROBLEM.

WAIT!!
I THINK I KNOW WHO THO CULPRIT IS!

HOY NARRATOR!
BOD-RIDDON BUDDY!

STOP USING OUR RIGHT NOW!!!

SO THO LAST PORSON USING YOU-KNOW-WHO STOPPOD.

QUICK AS A WINK, SHO
WAS OUT OF BOD AND ROADY
TO GO BACK TO WORK.

JUST IN TIMO FOR . . .

thE End.

EEEE
WEE
MY BABY... SHE WROTE ME A LETTER...
FOR E'S A JOLLY GOOD FELLOW...
WHERE'S THE PARTEE?
THIS IS THE SPOT!
WHAT KEY ARE WE IN?
E, OF COURSE!
WE ARE TOO FUN!
LET'S CHA-CHA!

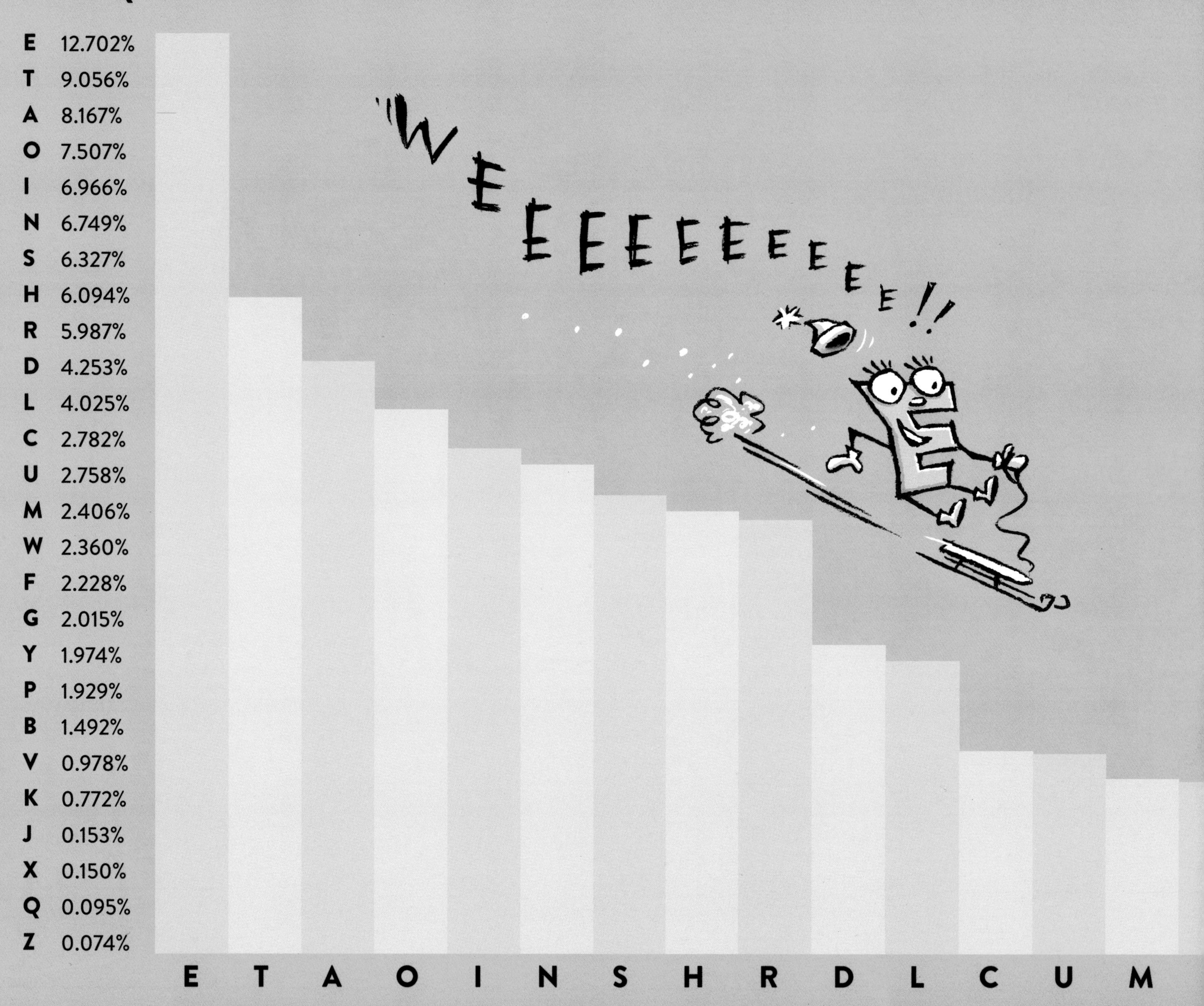
FREQUENCY OF USE IN THE ENGLISH LANGUAGE
E 12.702%
T 9.056%
A 8.167%
O 7.507%
I 6.966%
N 6.749%
S 6.327%
H 6.094%
R 5.987%
D 4.253%
L 4.025%
C 2.782%
U 2.758%
M 2.406%
W 2.360%
F 2.228%
G 2.015%
Y 1.974%
P 1.929%
B 1.492%
V 0.978%
K 0.772%
J 0.153%
X 0.150%
Q 0.095%
Z 0.074%
"WEEEEEEEEEEE!!
E T A O I N S H R D L C U M

SHE JUST DOESN'T LEARN!
G Y P B V K J X Q Z